MORE Would You Rather...

John Burningham

JONATHAN CAPE • LONDON

For Nells

Some other picture books by John Burningham

Picnic	*Mr Gumpy's Motor Car*	*Husherbye*
Borka	*Mr Gumpy's Outing*	*Granpa*
Tug of War	*Avocado Baby*	*Courtney*
Simp	*The Magic Bed*	*Humbert*
Aldo	*Whadayamean*	*Cloudland*
Come Away From the Water, Shirley	*Oi! Get Off Our Train*	*The Shopping Basket*
Would You Rather?	*Edwardo, the Horriblest Boy in the Whole Wide World*	*Time to Get Out of the Bath, Shirley*
Mouse House	*John Patrick Norman McHennessy*	*Motor Miles*

JONATHAN CAPE

UK | USA | Canada | Ireland | Australia
India | New Zealand | South Africa

Jonathan Cape is part of the Penguin Random House group of companies
whose addresses can be found at global.penguinrandomhouse.com.

www.penguin.co.uk   www.puffin.co.uk   www.ladybird.co.uk

Penguin
Random House
UK

First published 2018
001

Copyright © John Burningham, 2018
The moral right of the author has been asserted

Printed in China
A CIP catalogue record for this book is available from the British Library

ISBN: 978-0-857-55202-0

All correspondence to:
Jonathan Cape, Penguin Random House Children's,
80 Strand, London WC2R 0RL

MIX
Paper from
responsible sources
FSC® C018179

Would you rather . . .

help the bees make honey

or a rabbit dig a hole
in the ground?

Would it be worse to be punched
by a bad-tempered baby

or pushed over
by a badger?

Would you like to fly with the pelicans

or swim with
the fish?

Would it be worse if everyone talked about when you were a baby

or your mother did that
thing with her tissue?

Would you rather serve a meal
to a very polite rat

or a bad-mannered cat?

Would it be worse if a camel was sick down your neck,

an elephant made a terrible smell

or you fell over in a field
full of cows?

Would you like to
jump with
kangaroos

or swing in the trees
with monkeys?

Would it be worse to
break Granny's
favourite jug,

scratch
the car

or spill paint all
over the carpet?

Would you like

a tiger to tell you a tale,

a wizard to sing you a song,

a goose to cook your dinner

or a pig to push you along?

Would it be worse if
everybody laughed at you

or an eagle stole all your clothes?

Would you like to have

breakfast with bears,

lunch with a lion

or dinner with ducks?

Would it be worse
to be kissed by
Aunty Zelda

or a hippo with bad breath?

Would you like to
have a pet

koala bear,

vulture,

alligator

or sheep?

Would you rather go to
sleep on the moon,

with some birds in a nest . . .

or perhaps you would rather
just be in your own bed?